WISDOM

— TO —

REMEMBER

Life Advice from a Forgetful Fish

Disney · PIXAR
FINDING DORY

WISDOM
— TO —
REMEMBER

Life Advice from a Forgetful Fish

By Kristen L. Depken

Random House 🏠 New York

Sometimes it might
feel like you're
all alone ...

... with **no one** on your side ....

. . . and **no idea**
which way to turn.

Don't let
your worries
keep you
from moving
forward!

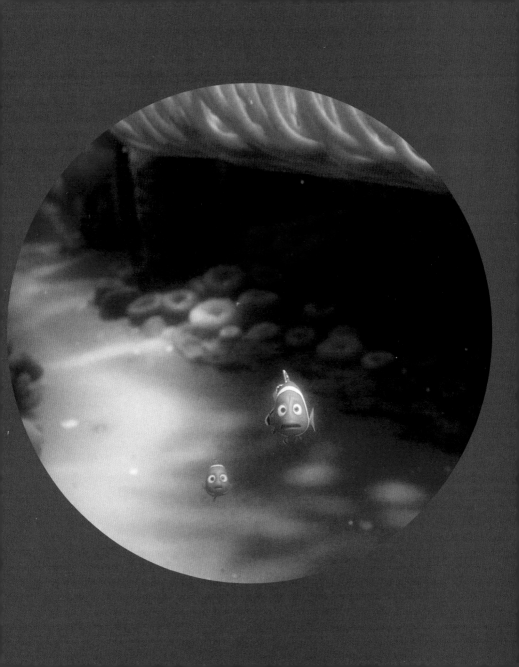

There's a
great big world
out there.

It might seem
scary at first.

Most new things do.

But you have
what it takes
to **soar**.

You're **smart** . . .

... kind ...

. . . and **determined**.

That's a winning combination!

So . . . **relax!**

Keep your **chin up.**

And be
positive.

Then share your joy with **others**.

Take in the **beauty** that's all around you.

Never underestimate the value of a **good education.**

Listen to your **teachers** . . .

WA...
LET IT BE...
TO ADHERE...

BOILING LIQUIDS IN GLAS...
AND MAY CAUSE GLAS...

TO PREVENT BOILING
WHICH IS TOO...
AN ENJOYA...

DO NOT U...
HEATER...
IN GLAS...

FILLING A...
THE CHA...

...oz

. . . but don't follow the **herd**.

Ask questions . . .

. . . and look to those who care about you for **advice**.

Don't take your friends for granted.

Stick up for them . . .

and **cheer them on**
every chance you get.

Be cautious.

But don't be afraid
to **explore**.

Have your own **opinions** . . .

. . . and learn to
accept criticism.

Be a leader...

. . . and give advice **gently**.

There may be times
when you **feel stuck** . . .

. . . and **lazy** . . .

. . . and all you want
to do is **hide**.

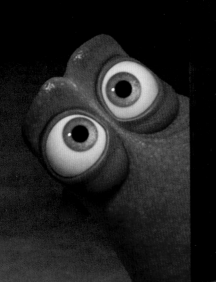

Don't panic!

Stay on track . . .

. . . and know when
to **ask for help**.

Volunteer to help others.

Point them in the
right direction.

And lend a **helping hand**
whenever you can.

Have **courage** even when you're most afraid.

Travel to new places.

Learn about those who
are different from you . . .

. . . and make friends in unexpected places.

You may not always **see** eye to eye . . .

. . . but you can learn to communicate.

Be a good role model.

Think outside the **bowl**.

Don't let anyone **pressure** you into something you're not comfortable with.

Don't be afraid to get your **hands dirty** . . .

. . . and always **clean up** after yourself.

Go to great lengths for your friends.

Stick together.

Remember that your family may not always **understand** you . . .

. . . but they will always
be there for you.

Life is full of surprises.

So hang in there!

And **enjoy** the journey.